LONE WOLF and CUB

by
KAZUO KOIKE
and
GOSEKI KOJIMA

cover by
MATT WAGNER

第33巻

小池一夫
小島剛夕

Kazuo Koike
STORY

Goseki Kojima
ART

Matt Wagner
COVER ILLUSTRATION

Dana Lewis, Alex Wald, Byron Erickson
ENGLISH ADAPTATION

Willie Schubert
LETTERING

Noreen Ryan
PRODUCTION

Byron Erickson EDITOR	**Rick Obadiah** PUBLISHER
Alex Wald ART DIRECTOR	**Kathy Kotsivas** OPERATIONS DIRECTOR
Mike McCormick PRODUCTION MANAGER	**Kurt Goldzung** SALES DIRECTOR
Rich Markow TRAFFIC MANAGER	**Bob Garcia** SENIOR EDITOR

Lone Wolf and Cub (Kozure Okami) © 1990 Kazuo Koike and Goseki Kojima.

English translation © 1990 First Publishing, Inc. and Global Communications Corporation.

Cover illustration © 1990 Matt Wagner.

Published monthly in the United States of America by First Publishing, Inc., 435 N. LaSalle, Chicago IL 60610, and Studio Ship, Inc. under exclusive license by Global Communications Corporation, Musashiya Building, 4th Floor, 27-10, Aobadai 1-Chome, Meguro-Ku, Tokyo, 153 Japan, owner of worldwide publishing rights to the property Lone Wolf and Cub.

Lone Wolf and Cub #33 (ISBN 0-915419-62-9) © 1990 First Publishing, Inc. and Global Communications Corporation. All rights reserved.

Price: $2.95 in the U.S. Subscription rates for 12 issues: $35.00 in the U.S., $40.00 in Canada, and $65.00 foreign rate. All payments must be in U.S. funds.

First printing, May 1990.

Separate Paths

其之三十六

大五郎絶唱

"YOU'VE DONE WELL, ITTO OGAMI. YOU'VE SUCCEEDED IN CARVING A *BLOODY* PATH THROUGH MY FORCES."

"BUT YOU'LL GO NO FURTHER."

"YOUR INFERNAL GUNS ARE USELESS NOW. YOU'VE LOST YOUR STYLE ALONG WITH YOUR SPEARS."

"EVEN YOUR SWORD DOTANUKI MUST BE AS NOTCHED AND BATTERED AS AN OLD SAW!"

HA HA HA! YOU'VE LURED ME INTO THE LONG GRASS SO YOU CAN USE IT IN PLACE OF WATER FOR YOUR SUIO WAVE-SLICING TECHNIQUE.

YOU HOPE TO CONCEAL THE DISTANCE BETWEEN ME AND YOUR BLADE, FORCING ME TO GUESS ABOUT YOUR UPWARD STROKE. BUT YOUR WAVE-SLICING STROKE IS CHILD'S PLAY TO ME!

WILL HE COME FROM THE LEFT, OR FROM THE RIGHT? I SUPPOSE THAT'S THE GREAT SECRET OF YOUR LITTLE SUIO SCHOOL...

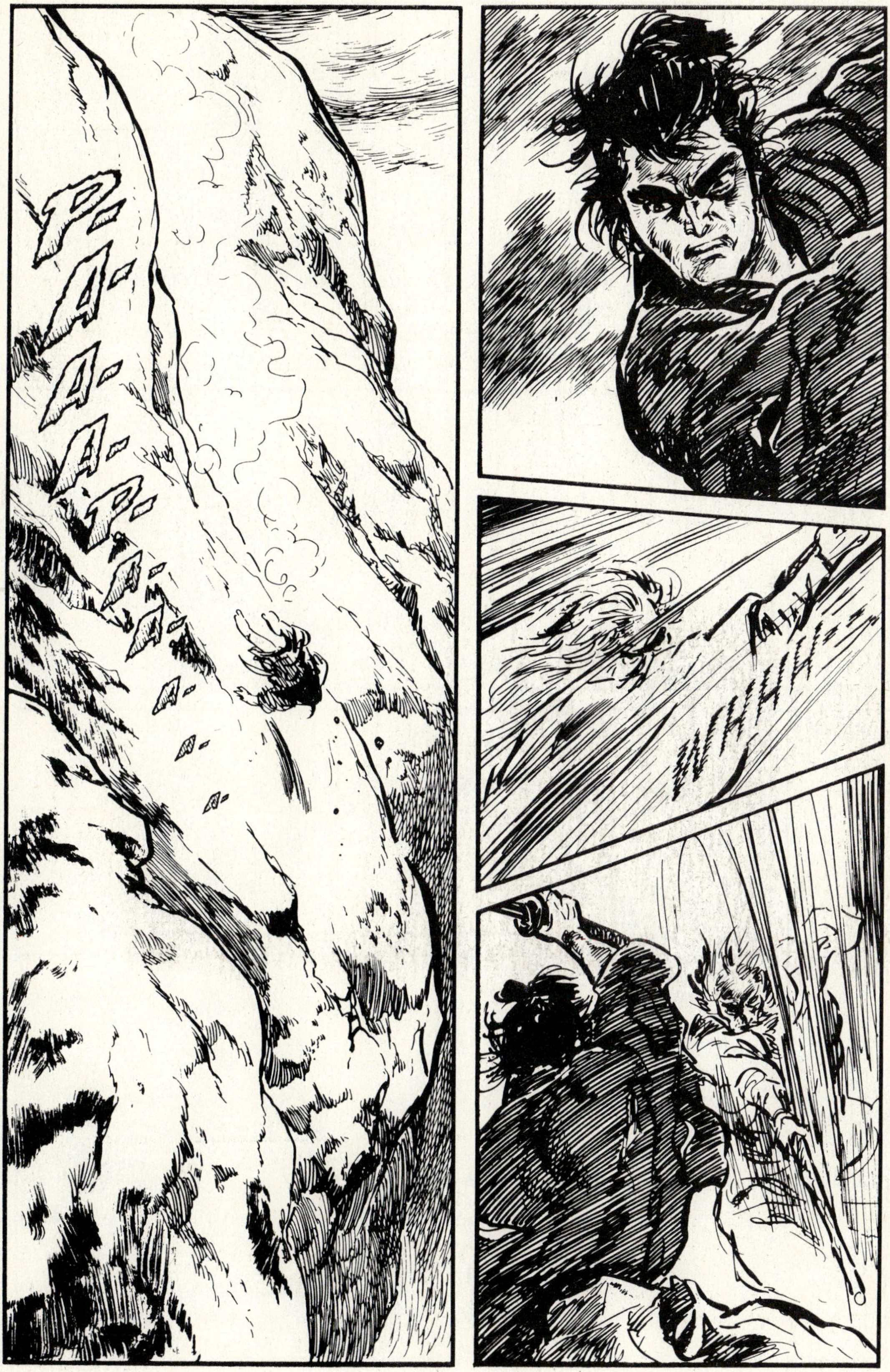
P-A-A-A-P-A-A-A-A-A-
WHHH--

THE GO-JOBAKO WAS IN THE BABY CART, MY LORD.

BRING IT TO ME.

DAMN YOU, OGAMI!

THE LETTER MUST BE HIDDEN ON HIM!

HURRY! FIND HIS BODY!

OUCH!

POKED YOURSELF AGAIN?

WAAAAH! WAAAAH!

THERE, THERE. NO NEED TO CRY ABOUT IT. LET'S TAKE A BREAK.

WAA... (sniff) (sniff)

SNRKK

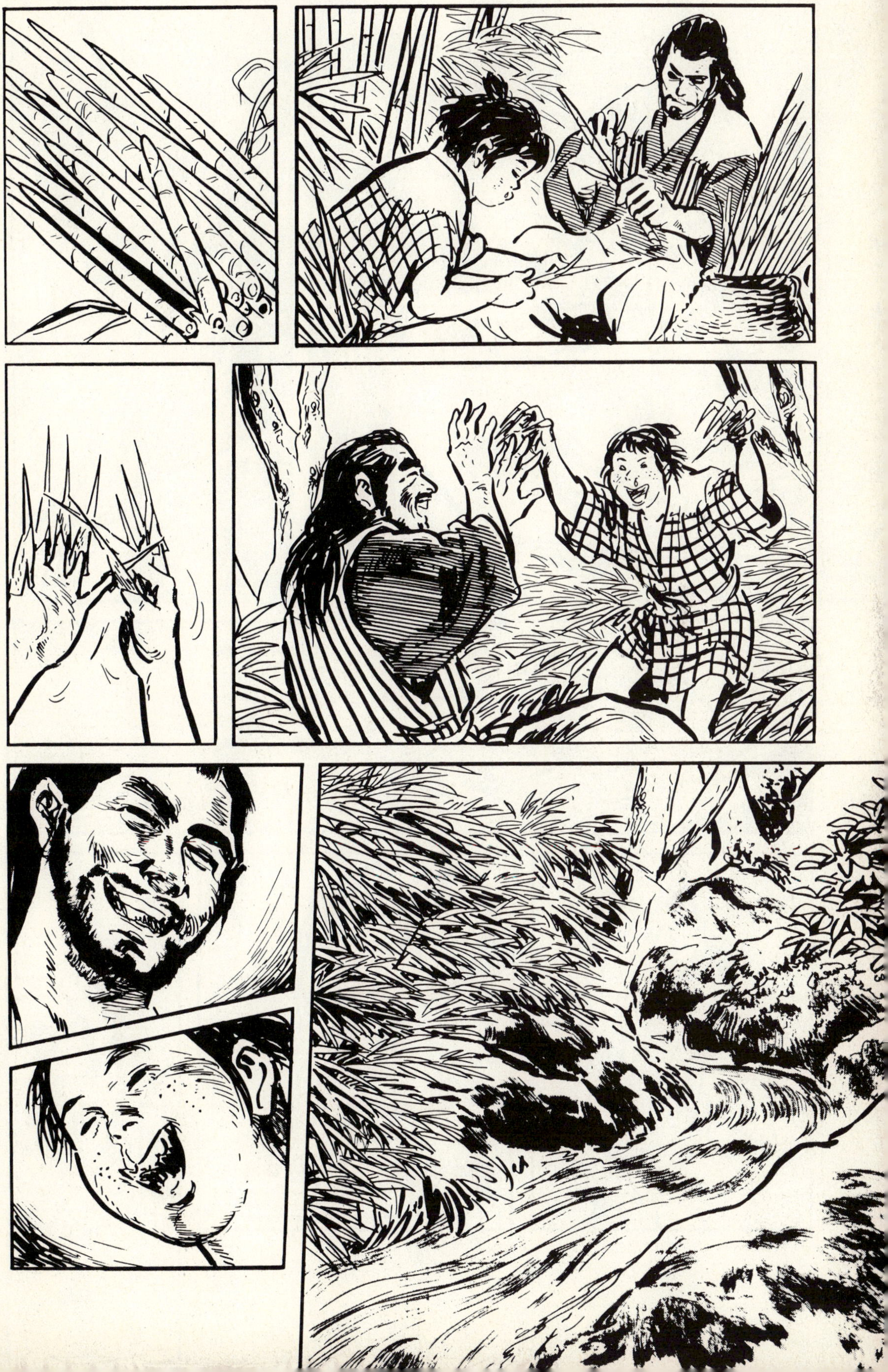

37

?!

AA!

YAAAAH!

MOSAKU! WHAT'S WRONG?

HE'S DEAD! HE'S DEAD!
HMPH!
HE'S DEAD!
NO, HE ISN'T DEAD. HE'LL BE ALL RIGHT.

HE AIN'T DEAD.

YEAH, HE AIN'T DEAD!

41

PAPA!

PAPA!

PAPA!

AH! YOU'VE COME TO, HAVE YOU? VERY GOOD.

YOU FELL OFF THE CLIFF. WE FOUND YOU, AND BROUGHT YOU BACK TO OUR HUT.

YOU HAVE NOTHING TO FEAR HERE.

PAPA!

WHOA! HOLD ON!

CALM DOWN! WHERE DO YOU THINK YOU'RE GOING?

PAPA!

YOU MUSN'T MOVE YET.

YOUR FATHER MUST HAVE MET WITH SOME *CALAMITY* ALSO...

...BUT THERE'S NO WAY WE CAN SEARCH FOR HIM IN THE DARK.

WE'LL HAVE TO WAIT UNTIL MORNING. DON'T WORRY, LAD, WE'LL FIND YOUR FATHER FOR YOU...

...I PROMISE.

....
....

THE WAY HE SITS, HIS MOVEMENTS, AND ABOVE ALL, THOSE *EYES*... HE MUST BE A SAMURAI CHILD! HE ANSWERS NO QUESTIONS, HIS LIPS ARE SEALED.

WHY HE'LL SAY NO MORE THAN "PAPA" I DON'T KNOW, BUT WHATEVER HAPPENED TO HIM MUST HAVE BEEN *TRAUMATIC* INDEED.

44

STILL, TO HAVE FALLEN OFF THAT CLIFF AND SUFFERED NO MORE THAN A FEW SCRAPES AND SCRATCHES...

...HE MUST HAVE BEEN BORN UNDER A RARE LUCKY STAR.

"IS ANYONE IN THERE?"

"WE'VE LOST OUR WAY."

"HARD LUCK, EH?"

"WE'VE NO WHERE TO GO."

"COULD YOU PUT US UP FOR THE NIGHT?"

"THIS IS A POOR PLACE, NOT GOOD FOR MUCH MORE THAN KEEPING OFF THE MORNING DEW. YET YOU ARE WELCOME HERE."

"WE THANK YOU."

FORGIVE US FOR ASKING, BUT WHY DO YOU LIVE IN THIS CRUDE MOUNTAIN HUT?

YOUR MANNER AND BEARING ARE NOT THOSE OF A MERE WOODCUTTER.

ARE YOU A RONIN?

IT'S BEEN SIX YEARS SINCE I GAVE UP MY LIFE AS A SAMURAI AND MOVED TO THESE MOUNTAINS.

NOW I EKE OUT A LIVING CHOPPING WOOD AND WORKING WITH BAMBOO. I GATHER THE MOUNTAIN PLANTS FOR FOOD. YOU NEED NOT TREAT ME OTHERWISE.

BUT WHY? SUCH AN UPSTANDING MAN AS YOURSELF...?

MY SON IS *RETARDED.*

I HAD HOPED FOR A STRONG HEIR, ONE WHO WOULD CARRY ON THE FAMILY LINE, BUT... THE FAULT LIES IN THE FATHER...

POOR CHILD.

WHEN WE LIVED IN TOWN, ALL THE NEIGHBORHOOD CHILDREN MADE FUN OF HIM. THE BOY WOULD COME HOME CRYING EVERY DAY. EVEN THE *LITTLE* CHILDREN WOULD PICK ON HIM.

HERE WE CAN LIVE QUIETLY, FATHER AND SON. I BEGGED MY LORD FOR LEAVE AND MOVED TO THIS SIMPLE HUT.

A PARENT MUST TAKE *RESPONSIBILITY* FOR THE LIFE OF HIS CHILD.

"OUR HAN IS POOR. WHEN I SOUGHT LEAVE AND RENOUNCED OUR HEREDITARY FAMILY STIPEND..."

"...IT WAS THAT MUCH LESS BURDEN ON OUR LORD."

"THEN, YOU DIDN'T BETRAY YOUR DEBT TO YOUR LORD BY LEAVING HIS SERVICE JUST TO CARE FOR YOUR OWN CHILD?"

"NO, I WILL NOT LIVE FOREVER. IT WOULD BE A *GREATER* BETRAYAL..."

"...TO LEAVE A RETARDED CHILD TO FOLLOW ME IN MY LORD'S SERVICE."

"I SEE."

"AND WHAT OF *THAT* BOY OVER THERE?"

"I SUSPECT YOU KNOW FAR MORE ABOUT HIM THAN I."

"YOUR ATTENTION AND HATRED HAVE BEEN FOCUSED ENTIRELY AT HIM SINCE YOU CAME IN."

HURM!

THAT'S WHY I RELATED THE STORY OF MY LIFE SO READILY WHEN YOU ASKED.

IF YOU UNDERSTAND MY FEELINGS FROM MY TALE, YOU'LL LEAVE NOW, WITHOUT ANOTHER WORD. NO MATTER WHAT THE CIRCUMSTANCES MAY BE...

...IT IS THE *DUTY* OF ONE ENTRUSTED WITH A CHILD TO RETURN HIM TO THE SIDE OF HIS PARENTS.

THAT BOY WAS ENTRUSTED TO ME BY HEAVEN...

....
....

...AND THE HATRED YOU BEAR FOR HIM IS *ABNORMAL!*

A MAN WHO HAS DEVOTED HIS ENTIRE LIFE TO HIS CHILD *CANNOT* STAND IDLY BY!

SHOULD YOU TRY TO HARM THAT BOY, I MUST FOLLOW THE WILL OF HEAVEN AND DEFEND HIM TO THE DEATH!

POP!

SEIZE HIM!

BUT WHAT ABOUT...?

IT CAN'T BE HELPED. KILL HIM!

WHOOOSH!

SWISH!

WAAAH! WAAAH! Uhnmm!

WAAA...

MOSAKU! TAKE THE BOY AND RUN AWAY!

DO YOU UNDERSTAND ME?! PROTECT THAT BOY!
WAAAH!
AAAA
WAAAH!
BRAT!
STOP!
EEE-YAAAH!

55

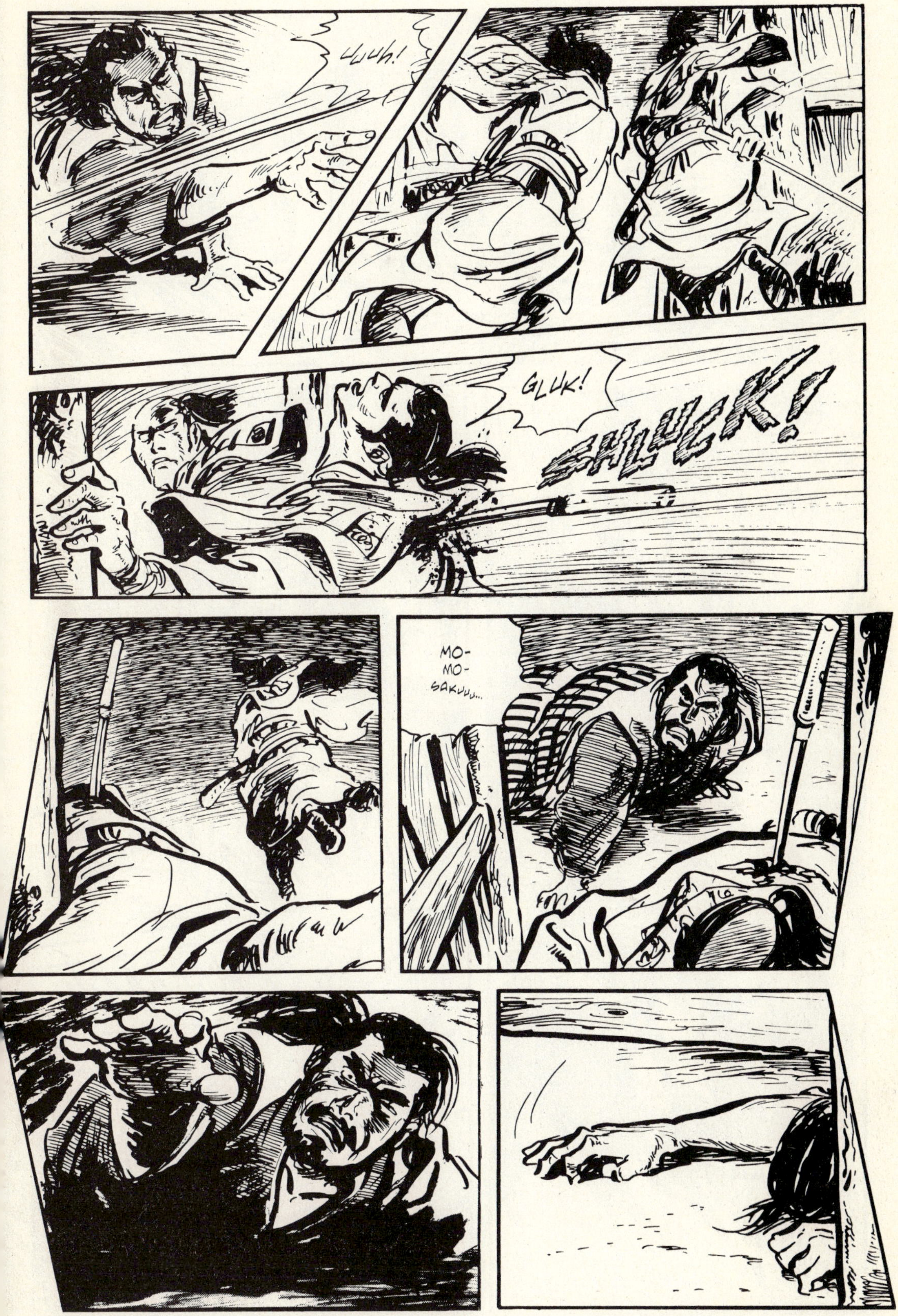
UUUH!
GLUK!
SHLUCK!
MO-
MO-
SAKUUU...

WAAAAAAAAH!
AAAAAAAAAH!
WAAAH!
GET OUT OF MY WAY, YOU BRAT!
WAAAH!
WAAAAAAAH!

HEY! WATCH OU...

HOU LITTLE...

WAAAAAA...

He was a boy who did not know tears...

...a silent child who showed no emotions.

A child of fate, tragically used to the world of slaughter that surrounded him.

It was not...

(sniff) (snuf)

...out of fear that he wept.

It was not out of loneliness.

Not those tears. For the first time in his short life, the child wept in sadness.

LETTERS

Dear Ms. Bennett,

Your work schedule is probably as hectic as mine, so perhaps you will sympathize with one who uses his lunch hour to forcibly break (all too temporarily) from a very busy day. As a consequence, I spend this brief quiet time doing something I enjoy.

During one of these lunch breaks I was reading the latest issue of *Lone Wolf and Cub*. A co-worker noticed what I was doing and was incredulous. "You're a university-educated physicist and you read comic books?"

I paused for a moment to think of an explanation.

Lone Wolf is certainly not a standard "comic book." More accurately, it is "visual literature." In fact, *Lone Wolf* is the only story in this format I have ever read. "I read it for the story," I replied. "I can't put it down."

"Why?" was the predictable response.

Again, another pause. "Do you like your job?" I asked.

"Yeah, I guess so. It's a living, right?"

"Do you like to drive to work, pay taxes, talk to people you don't care for, mow your lawn, and all the petty stuff in life?"

"Well, no, not really."

"Yet you bought into the system. You don't really like it, yet you participate."

It was his turn to pause.

"That's kind of what *Lone Wolf* is about," I continued. "Here's a guy who was very respected in his profession. He was part of the system. In fact, it could be argued the system flourished in part because of him. Then he got screwed and chucked the system. He rebelled, and decided to live his life by his own rules, not someone else's. Now that same system is out to crush him, but as long as he's true to himself, he stays one step ahead of the game. The trick is...for how long? Is there an end to his quest? Is it the quest for its own sake and not the goal that's important? Are there others who feel the same way? Can he help them? Can they help him?"

Again, another pause.

"His society and ours aren't that different. Oh, sure, there are niggling differences in language, behavior, philosophy, etc., but no entrenched system, social or political, tolerates a rebel. Ours doesn't. You wear the corporate uniform, drive the socially acceptable car, eat the socially acceptable food, watch TV, don't talk too much or too loudly (not that anyone listens, anyway), or you're out."

"But that's why you're not part of the management staff," he pointed out.

"And that's why I'm happy," I answered. I finished my lunch in peace.

Bret Ryan Rudnick
P.O. Box 363
Wayland, MA 01778

Then again, it could be argued that the system in effect at the time of Lone Wolf and Cub *was the code of bushido, a system that dictated every aspect of an adherent's life. Far from chucking it and going his own way, Ogami's goal could be seen as the enforcement of the real meaning of that system on his enemies. In other words, the Lone Wolf as the last true "company man."*

Comments, rebuttals, or responses, anyone?

— *Byron Erickson*

OTHER FINE BOOKS FROM FIRST

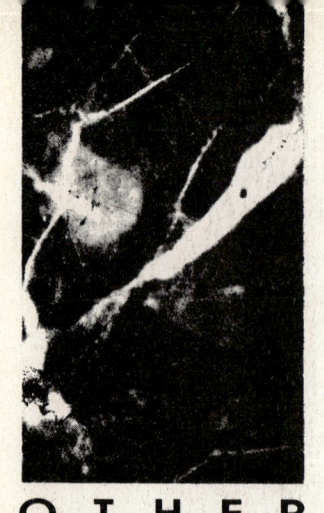

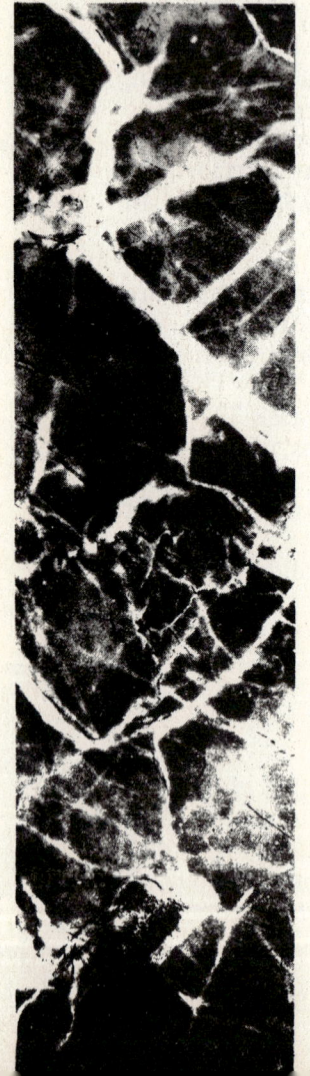

TRADE PAPERBACKS
FOR CHILDREN
The Enchanted Apples of Oz ($7.95)
The Secret Island of Oz ($7.95)
The Ice King of Oz ($7.95)
The Forgotten Forest of Oz ($8.95)

FOR ALL AGES
Beauty and the Beast: Portrait of Love ($5.95)
Beauty and the Beast: Night of Beauty ($5.95)
Beowulf ($6.95)
Elric of Melniboné ($14.95)
Elric: Sailor on the Seas of Fate ($14.95)
Hawkmoon: The Jewel in the Skull ($9.95)
Hexbreaker: A Badger Graphic Novel ($8.95)
The Original Nexus ($7.95)
The Next Nexus ($9.95)
Teenage Mutant Ninja Turtles®, Books 1-4 ($9.95 each)

FOR MATURE READERS
American Flagg!: Hard Times ($11.95)
American Flagg!: Southern Comfort ($11.95)
American Flagg!: State of the Union ($11.95)
Team Yankee: The Graphic Novel ($12.95)
Demon Knight: A Grimjack Graphic Novel ($8.95)
Time^2: The Satisfaction of Black Mariah ($7.95)

COMIC MAGAZINES
Badger ($1.95)
Dreadstar ($1.95)
Grimjack ($1.95)
Lone Wolf and Cub ($3.25)
Nexus ($1.95)

CLASSICS ILLUSTRATED
The Raven and Other Poems by Edgar Allan Poe ($3.75)
Great Expectations ($3.75)
Through The Looking-Glass ($3.75)
Moby Dick ($3.75)
Hamlet ($3.75)
The Scarlet Letter ($3.75)
The Count of Monte Cristo ($3.75)
Dr. Jekyll and Mr. Hyde ($3.75)
The Adventures of Tom Sawyer ($3.75)

First Publishing trade paperbacks, comics, and other products are available in finer bookstores and all comic retail stores throughout the country. To order individual trade paperbacks send cover price plus $1.50 for postage and handling; or for further information about comic magazine subscriptions write: First Publishing, 435 N. LaSalle Street, Chicago, IL 60610.